Contents

THE GREAT FIRE
A City in Flames

Ann Turnbull
Illustrated by Akbar Ali

A & C BLACK
AN IMPRINT OF BLOOMSBURY
LONDON   NEW DELHI   NEW YORK   SYDNEY

For my mother

First published 2013 by A & C Black
an imprint of Bloomsbury Publishing Plc
50 Bedford Square, London WC1B 3DP

www.bloomsbury.com

ISBN 978-1-4081-8686-2

A CIP catalogue for this book is available from the British Library.

This book is produced using paper that is made from wood
grown in managed, sustainable forests. It is natural, renewable
and recyclable. The logging and manufacturing processes conform
to the environmental regulations of the country of origin.

Printed by CPI Group (UK) Ltd, Croydon CR0 4YY

3 5 7 9 10 8 6 4 2

 **I**

GOLD AND DIAMONDS

"Sam!" his master called. "Come – look at this!"

Sam was sweeping the passage. He put down his broom and went into Paul Giraud's workshop.

André was already there. He gave Sam an unfriendly look – a look that said: *I'm your master's son. Don't you come pushing in here.*

But Master Giraud encouraged Sam to come in. "See! It's finished."

"Oh!" exclaimed Sam in delight.

On the table lay a necklace of gold, inlaid with blue enamel. From the chain, which sparkled with diamonds, hung a pendant in the shape of a ribbon bow, entwined with flowers. The folds of the blue ribbon were so lifelike that Sam almost believed it would drape across his hand if he picked it up. Tiny diamonds were set all along the ribbon edges and a larger one was set in the centre of each of the flowers. Sparks of light sprang from the diamonds and made everything glitter.

Sam had watched Master Giraud making the enamel, grinding granules of blue glass till they were a fine powder. Occasionally he would let Sam have a go. Sam liked feeling the glass crush and break and seeing the pure colour appear. And he enjoyed being in the workshop while André was out, at school.

"It's perfect," declared André.

"And it's important," said his father. "This is the most beautiful and expensive piece I have ever been asked to make. And Master Harrington's friends will see it, and so more customers will want my work."

Sam knew the necklace was for the new young wife of a wealthy merchant.

"Tonight I will finish and polish it, and place it in its casket," said Paul Giraud.

"Then tomorrow we will go to church and give thanks. And on Monday morning I will deliver it to Thomas Harrington. You shall come with me, André, before you go to school."

André smiled.

Sam, of course, would not go to the merchant's house. That honour was only for André, who was to follow his father into the family jewellery business.

Sam was a servant. His former master, William Kemp, had died of plague a year ago, and Sam, along with his dog, Budge, had been taken in by the Girauds.

The Girauds had four children: thirteen-year-old Thérèse; two much younger girls, Marie and Anne; and André, who was eleven – a year older than Sam.

What Master and Mistress Giraud hadn't known was that Sam and André already knew each other and that they were enemies. Sam and his friends used to bully André because he was scrawny, and French, and lame. Sam had pushed André over in the street and made him look a fool. Now André had Sam as a servant in his home and he took every opportunity to get his own back.

They left the workshop, and Sam returned to his sweeping. But soon he heard

André call from upstairs: "Sam! *Venez ici! Vite!*"

André was London-born and had never been to France, but he spoke both English and French. He deliberately gave orders to Sam in French so that he could call Sam an idiot when he didn't understand.

But Sam was learning. He'd been there long enough now to recognise some words, although he couldn't read or write – even in English. He ran upstairs, to André's bedchamber.

André rattled off another stream of French. Sam wanted to shout, "Speak English!" but he was only a servant, so he

simply gave André a blank look and kept his mouth shut. It would do no good to get into trouble with the Girauds. Where would he go if they threw him out?

"My prayer-book, stupid!" exclaimed André. "I can't find it."

Sam rummaged around. The small room had little enough in it, so the prayer-book should have been easy to find. He suspected that André had hidden it. "It's not here," he said.

"Oh! No, I remember now," said André – and Sam knew he was doing this on purpose – "I left it in the kitchen. Go down and get it for me."

Sam's patience snapped. "Of course!" he said, glancing at André's left leg, the one with the built-up shoe. "*I* can run down in no time."

He was rewarded by a look of fury on André's face, and scampered downstairs, grinning.

The kitchen was full of busy women – Mistress Giraud, Thérèse and the maid, Amy – preparing food for supper.

Budge was there, too, involved in a spat with Bijou, the cat. Bijou stood in front of the fire. There was a ridge of fur along her back and her round yellow eyes were fixed on Budge, who had slunk into a corner.

"Poor Budge," muttered Sam, reaching to stroke his dog. "We both have enemies, don't we?"

"Sam!" said Mistress Giraud. "Don't waste time. Here – take out these scraps. And when you come back there are shoes to be cleaned."

"I was looking for André's prayer-book," said Sam.

Mistress Giraud huffed with impatience. "Well, it's not here!"

Sam took the peelings out, then went back upstairs.

André lay on the bed, reading his prayer-book.

"It was under the coverlet," he said, with a malicious glint in his eyes.

This is stupid, Sam thought. *I've said sorry – sort of. But he never leaves me alone.*

* * *

Later that evening Sam went to bed in his little curtained alcove on the first-floor landing. It was a tiny space, but he liked it. Budge was allowed to sleep there too. And there was a window on the landing that was left open in hot weather.

The window faced east, and a strong wind was blowing in – as warm as the blast from an oven. All over the house, doors rattled and banged, and the curtain across Sam's alcove billowed like a ship's sail. Despite all this, he slept.

He woke in the dead of night. Budge was whimpering, and Sam could hear, in the distance, the discordant sound of church bells ringing the chimes backwards. He knew this was the alarm signal.

Sam got up and went to the window. He stared out over the yard and rooftops.

It was probably a fire. There were always fires, especially in this hot summer when the old wooden houses were as dry as tinder.

But he couldn't see anything. It must be a long way off.

He went back to bed, and fell asleep.

2

FIRE!

When Sam woke again it was light. The wind was still banging the shutters, and he could hear footsteps along the passage and on the stairs.

He sprang up, feeling guilty. He should be downstairs by now, clearing the ashes, feeding Bijou and Budge, and doing any other jobs Amy or Mistress Giraud gave him.

In a room nearby Mistress Giraud and Thérèse were dressing the younger girls for church. He could hear six-year-old Marie chattering, and the little one, Anne, being chased and caught. All the church bells were ringing this morning, and he could no longer make out an alarm peal.

Sam pulled on his clothes and ran downstairs, Budge racing ahead of him.

Amy was already in the kitchen, cutting bread.

"You're late!" she said. "Get the fire raked out. And have you cleaned the shoes?"

There were five pairs of Giraud shoes to clean each day. There would have been six, but André would not let Sam touch his shoes, and insisted on cleaning them himself.

"I did them last night," said Sam. "Amy, did you hear the alarm peal in the night?"

"No." Amy frowned, and opened the back door. There was a faint smell of smoke.

"Probably a fire down east," said Amy. "It's a long way off. So many fires we've had this summer."

"Miaou!" interrupted Bijou. She wound herself around Sam's legs.

Sam found yesterday's meat scraps and divided them between Bijou's bowl and Budge's. The two animals ate warily, watching each other.

Sam went into the scullery and splashed water from a pail over his face and hands.

"And put a clean shirt on for the Lord's day!" called Amy.

Soon after, they were on their way to church.

The Girauds lived in Foster Lane, off Cheapside, and their church was further east, in Threadneedle Street. As they walked along Cheapside the smell of smoke became stronger, and now they could hear the alarm peal. People in the street were talking about a fire blazing all down Fish Street Hill that had spread to the houses on London Bridge.

Inside the church they were shut off from whatever was happening outside. Most of the service was in French, so Sam daydreamed and gazed around. He had learned when to stand up, sit down, kneel, or murmur, "Amen".

I wonder if we can go and see the fire, he thought. *I'd like to see the bridge on fire!*

When they came out of the church they saw people running up the street shouting that the bridge was half burned and the fire was spreading westwards along the wharfage.

"There's a gale blowing from the east," said Paul Giraud. He looked concerned.

"Shall we go and see the fire?" asked André, his eyes bright with interest.

Marie exclaimed, "Oh, please, Papa! Please!"

To Sam's delight Paul Giraud said, "We'll go down here a little way..."

Many people had the same idea, and the street was crowded. As they drew nearer the river Sam saw smoke ahead.

At the bottom of the hill a group of men passed by, hauling a fire-squirt on its cart, and then some more rushed past with fire-hooks and ladders. Cries of alarm rose faintly from lower down, by the river.

Mistress Giraud exclaimed, "No further!

Husband – Amy and I will take the children home. The fire is spreading. It's dangerous. And we should not block the streets."

"Yes, you go straight home with the girls," agreed Master Giraud. "I must find out what is happening. André will be safe with me."

Sam attached himself quickly to Master Giraud and André. He was eager to see the fire. The two groups separated, and Sam heard Marie complaining as she was hustled away.

At the bottom of the hill they came suddenly on a view of the waterfront – and there, to their left, was a terrible and thrilling scene. On their side, the northern bank, the bridge was blazing. Several of the houses built along its length were already blackened shells, and flames were shooting up to the sky, sending smoke and burning sparks along the waterfront.

Paul Giraud looked shocked. "The timber warehouses will catch fire," he said. "It will only take one spark."

When the smoke briefly cleared they saw a stream of people moving along the wharfage with bundles and bags and handcarts full of possessions – even chairs and cabinets, Sam noticed in amazement. Crowds congregated at Old Swan Stairs. From there a flotilla of small boats laden with people was making its way to the Southwark side. Nearer the fire they saw several men operating one of the squirts, sending a jet of water up to the first floor of a burning house.

"I had no idea it was so bad!" exclaimed Paul Giraud.

One of the other Frenchmen from the church said, "They're saying it's a revenge attack. For Terschelling."

Sam knew his country was at war with Holland. Only a few weeks ago there had been huge celebrations in London over the burning of a town on the Dutch island of Terschelling by the English navy. There was a procession with the mayor and aldermen in their robes of office, and drums and flags, and fireworks in the evening. Sam had been as excited as anyone. But could this be revenge by Dutch agents?

They listened as speculation flew around the group of onlookers.

"Where did the fire start?"

"In a bakery, they say, in Pudding Lane."

"An accident, then?"

"Or a fireball thrown by some foreign agent. I heard a Frenchman was seen around there."

A look of anxiety crossed Paul Giraud's face. "Boys," he said quickly, "we must go home – now. If foreigners are suspected, none of us will be safe."

He began to lead them back up the hill.

"But we are not Dutch!" André protested. "The war is with Holland."

"Dutch, French, Walloons, Catholics – all will be suspects now."

"We are not Catholics either," said André, frowning.

"The English are always quick to turn against anyone different," said his father.

Sam thought guiltily of the way he and his friends in Friday Street used to set upon the French boys. *It's true*, he thought.

Paul Giraud hustled them quickly back uphill, then along Cheapside towards Foster Lane. The sounds of fire and confusion faded behind them.

As they turned into Foster Lane, Sam saw how relieved his master was to be back at his home; and he thought of the costly and beautiful necklace, now finished, and hidden away in Paul Giraud's workshop.

Neighbours were out on the street, talking about the fire and the rumours of a Dutch attack.

"It'll be under control soon," one of the goldsmiths said. "There are always fires in this hot weather. And it's a long way from here."

But that evening the wind changed direction. By the time the Girauds were on their way to bed it was blowing from the south, towards the heart of the city – and their home.

3

COME STRAIGHT HOME

Next morning it was dark outside and the house smelled of smoke. Budge was whining, and Bijou crouched in the kitchen with her haunches sticking up and a wild look in her yellow eyes.

"You both know something's wrong, don't you?" said Sam as he followed the Girauds outside, into Foster Lane. All the neighbours were there, talking in anxious voices.

Clouds of black smoke filled the sky. The air was hot. To the south-east they saw flames, and from the close-packed buildings came a deep, crackling roar.

It's like a hungry beast, thought Sam. He heard an explosion and saw a distant flash of fire.

An endless stream of people was moving past the end of the road, carrying bundles, bags and babies, holding small children by the hand, dragging carts full of belongings – all of them hurrying westwards, away from the city.

"We must pack up and leave!" cried Mistress Pryce, the goldsmith's wife from next door.

"And go where?" another woman asked.

"To the fields! Lincoln's Inn. St Giles. Or Hatton Garden."

Sam felt excited at the idea of camping in the fields and he could see that André and his sisters did, too. But their mother was distraught. "Husband, what do you think? Must we leave?"

"Not yet," said Paul Giraud. "I heard there were looters in Cheapside. We can't leave our home and workplace open to them. Before we do anything else I must deliver that necklace to Thomas Harrington."

Sam knew the necklace was packed and ready to deliver. It lay in its small casket on a bed of white silk, safely stowed away in the workshop. André and his father had both dressed in their best clothes this morning, to impress the merchant. André wore a new dark red doublet.

Little Anne began to cough.

"Come inside, children," urged Mistress Giraud. "This smoke is bad for you."

Sam followed reluctantly. He could hear shouting or chanting from Cheapside and wondered what was happening there.

Paul Giraud left the boys in the workshop and went out to investigate.

The sounds became much louder, and Sam realised that an angry mob was approaching. Soon it was outside – in Foster Lane. He heard banging, the sound of breaking glass, and screams.

Paul Giraud burst into the workshop.

"Close the shutters!" he cried.

Sam and André sprang to obey him. They fastened the wooden shutters, then followed him to the front of the house.

Sam heard chanting: "Frogs out! Frogs out! Frogs out!"

He felt afraid. But he was part of this family now. If they were Frogs, then so was he. He'd fight with them.

He and André ran to help Thérèse and Mistress Giraud, who were racing around, closing and barring every door and window.

"Marie! Anne! Upstairs! Thérèse – go with them! Now!" shouted Mistress Giraud. She and her husband began hauling a large wooden chest across the front entrance, which led into their shop.

Heavy blows battered the door.

"Come out, Frenchman! Out! Out!"

With each "out!" the door shuddered.

Paul Giraud shouted, "Sam! Take the necklace! Hide it under your clothes!"

Sam was surprised. *Why me?* he thought. But he ran to the workshop and grabbed the little casket.

André could not move as fast as Sam. He hobbled in behind him, furious. "*I should hide it! Give it to me!*"

Paul Giraud burst in, breathless.

"The door is blocked, but we don't have long," he gasped. "Sam, hide it, quickly!"

"But why – ?" began André.

His father took hold of André by the shoulders and said earnestly, "André, it's safer with Sam. Listen, we must not lose the necklace. It must be taken to Master Harrington now, or these thugs will steal it. Can I trust you to deliver it?"

Sam saw André's eyes light up.

"Yes! Of course!"

"Take Sam with you – "

Sam nodded eagerly, but André shook his head. "I don't need him!"

"Two will be safer," his father insisted. "*You* must deliver it, as my son and representative. But let Sam carry the casket. He's less likely to be attacked and robbed." He looked anxious for a moment. "Take the dog, too. You know the house, in Lothbury? The one with the lion carving?"

"Yes."

"Go out through the yard, and along the backs of the houses and up past Goldsmiths' Hall. Then straight along to Lothbury."

"I know the way!" André was impatient
to be gone.

The banging from the blocked door was
growing louder and louder.

"Stay together," his father said urgently.

"It's no distance, and well away from the fire. Deliver the casket and come straight back."

Both boys nodded.

A crash, followed by screams and yells, told them that the door had been forced open.

Paul Giraud sprang up.

"Go now," he whispered. "And remember – come straight home!"

4

FIREFIGHTERS

Sam and André took Budge and went out through the back gate. They hurried along the alley. From the street came shouts and sounds of fighting.

"Papa will see them off," said André fiercely. But Sam could tell he was anxious for his family.

To Sam's relief, no one took any notice of the two of them. The necklace was not heavy, but when he thought of its value –

not only the gold and diamonds, but Paul Giraud's exquisite workmanship – it became a weight he wished he didn't have to carry.

He was glad when André said, "There it is!" and he saw, ahead of them, a grand house with a lion's head carved above the door.

They walked up to the entrance.

André knocked and turned to Sam. "Give me the casket!" he commanded.

I wasn't going to keep it! Sam thought indignantly. But he said nothing, and handed it over.

"You and Budge can wait outside," said André, as the door opened.

Sam moved away, but not before he'd seen that the grand hall of Master Harrington's house was piled high with boxes, chests and crates. *Everyone is leaving the city*, he thought. *We'll all be camping in the fields together soon – even Mistress Harrington in her beautiful necklace.*

"Did he like the necklace?" Sam asked, when André came out. He wished he could have seen the man's face when he opened the casket.

"Yes," replied André. "He was very pleased, and thanked me. I told him about the rioters in our street and he sent a man to summon the militia."

A distant crash and a sound like thunder caused cries of alarm in the street. The boys stared, awestruck, at the black smoke billowing up to the south.

"We'll go down to the Exchange," said André. "We might see more from there."

Sam knew he should protest. Master Giraud had told them to come straight back. And yet it wasn't far out of their way, and he too wanted to see what was happening.

"Come on, Budge," he said.

They went down Bartholomew Lane and past the back of the Royal Exchange. They knew this area. The family's church was nearby.

"Down here!" called André. And instead of taking the way home through Poultry and Cheapside, he turned down one of the lanes that led south, towards the river.

Here the smoke was thicker. It stung their eyes. Budge strained at the lead and whimpered.

"We should go back," said Sam. "We'll be covered in soot and your father will know." *And André will make sure I get the blame,* he thought.

Suddenly flames sprang up into the sky ahead, followed by a tower of smoke that rolled down over the boys, black and choking. Shouts of alarm mingled with the crunch and crackle of the fire.

Then they heard screams: "Help! Help me!"

They stared through the thinning smoke. At the far end of a passageway a tall house was on fire. A woman with a baby in her arms was shouting from an upstairs window, and down below people had begun to gather.

"What can they do?" gasped André.

The boys hurried closer.

Now several people were holding up a large sheet. The woman hesitated, then – with a shriek – flung the baby out of the window. Sam saw it land in the sheet and be lifted up by a bystander.

By the time the woman had jumped down, and was holding the wailing baby, Sam and André were in the thick of the crowded street, among the firefighters.

"Don't just stand there!" a man shouted at Sam. He passed him an empty bucket.

"Stay, Budge," commanded Sam. He took the bucket, handed it to a woman beside him, and seized the next one as it came along. André joined in on his other side.

Now they were part of a double chain of firefighters. Some men had dug into the street and opened a water pipe. From there water was passed quickly along the line, emptied, and the buckets sent back to the pipe. Everyone was busy.

"Keep going! Faster! Faster!"

Those at the front threw bucket after bucket of water into the burning house. But they were losing. Flames burst from the upper windows, where the water couldn't reach.

Sam was tired. They were getting nowhere. Then, just as he felt like giving up, a cheer rose from the firefighters. Some militia men had appeared, shouting, "Make way! Make way!" Sam saw that they were pulling a cart with a water squirt on it.

Three men operated the squirt. Sam watched as it sucked up water from the pipe, and was then swivelled around to squirt a jet of water that went straight in through one of the blazing upper windows.

Buckets of water continued to be passed along, the squirt was refilled, and soon the fire was almost under control.

At last there were no more flames to be seen, although they could hear the never-ending roar of the fire all around. But the house – wet, blackened and smoking – was saved.

The men with the squirt moved on, and the firefighters threw down their buckets and cheered and hugged one another. Sam picked up Budge's lead as people began walking away.

André said, "We must get back. My father will be angry."

They turned to go. At that moment flames shot from the windows of a house in front of them. Sam saw green and gold embroidered hangings flare up, blacken and fall.

"It was a fireball!"

A man and woman rushed out of the front door, the man shouting, "The room burst into flames around us! There was no fire in our house before that. A fire-raiser has done this!"

The people in the street looked around, and Sam suddenly felt frightened. These people suspected arson – and foreigners.

"It's him!" a woman exclaimed. She pointed at André. "That French boy! I saw him! He threw something!"

"I didn't!" protested André. "I've been helping!" He looked terrified.

"He's lying! Arrest him!"

A man moved to seize André, but Sam sprang in front of him and shouted, "Leave him alone! We were firefighting! You saw us. We were in the chain!"

He turned to the others. "You know it wasn't him. You saw us passing buckets!"

It made no difference. They wanted a culprit. A foreigner. And André looked the part. Sam pushed past the man, grabbed André's arm, and pulled him out of reach.

"Quick!" he shouted. "Run, André! Run!"

5

ESCAPE

"Keep together!"

"I can't – "

Crowds of people surged up the road, separating the two boys. Sam, with Budge's lead wound around his wrist, caught only an occasional glimpse of André's red doublet. Sam glanced over his shoulder. Were those their pursuers back there? Yes! That man, glaring, calling to others behind him – he was one.

"Come on, Budge!" Sam seized the chance to duck and weave through the throng and shake the man off.

But now where was André? Sam could no longer see the red doublet anywhere. Had their enemies caught him? Or was he hiding?

"André!" he called. But there was no answer.

Smoke filled the street, and Sam realised for the first time that in their hurry to escape they had run downhill, towards the fire. Ahead of him was a whole row of blazing houses. No one was trying to put out the flames any more. Instead, people were intent on escaping with their possessions. The flow of refugees was all uphill – against him.

And still he could not see André.

"I've lost him," he told Budge. "And I was supposed to be looking after him. 'Two will be safer', Master Giraud said."

Two would also be company. He felt frightened, alone in the burning city.

He looked around. An alley led off to the left. Could André have gone that way? He turned down it, saw an open doorway, and peered into the dark interior.

"André?" he shouted.

"Sam! Is that you?" The faint voice came from deep inside the building.

"Yes!" Sam felt a huge sense of relief.

He led Budge into the empty shop. It was even darker in there than in the smoky street outside. He trampled on broken glass and bumped into overturned furniture.

Sam realised that this place had been ransacked by looters and for the first time he wondered what might have happened to the Girauds, back in Foster Lane.

"Where are you, André?" he called.

"Down here!"

In the dim light Sam noticed some steps leading to a storage room.

As he hurried down, Budge bounded ahead of him, and the dog's lead slipped out of Sam's hand and caught around his ankles as it fell to the ground.

Sam tripped and fell off the unguarded side of the steps, landing in a heap on the floor with Budge. Pain shot through his left arm. He cried out. Budge whimpered and nuzzled him.

André's concerned face came into view. "What have you done?"

"My arm – I think it might be broken." Sam felt sick and faint.

"Try moving it," said André.

"Aaargh! I can't! It hurts."

"We'll need a bone-setter, if it's broken."

Sam winced. "Maybe it isn't."

"Are they still following us – those people?"

"I don't think so."

"I'm sorry – I should have come up the steps to you," said André. "But I was so frightened. I felt safer down here." His voice wobbled. "You were good to speak up for me. I'm glad you're here, Sam."

Sam nodded. "Me, too. But we need to get out. There are houses on fire up the road."

"Could I make a sling for you? I could tear a strip off my shirt..."

It hurt to bend the arm, but Sam gritted his teeth and allowed André to put it into the makeshift sling.

"That should keep it steady," said André,
"till we can get it set."

"Thanks." Sam felt faint again.

Budge licked him, and he cuddled the dog with his good arm.

He was struggling to his feet when a whoosh and roar shook the building, sending a cloud of dust down onto them from the ceiling.

"What was that?" cried André.

"I don't know. But we should get out – now!"

6

TRAPPED

They rushed up the steps to the
ransacked shop. Budge ran ahead – then ran
back, whimpering.

Smoke was pouring into the shop
through the open doorway, and in the smoke
they saw the flicker of flames.

The boys stared at each other, and Sam
saw his own terror reflected in André's eyes.

They ran frantically to and fro, blinded
by the smoke. The front of the shop began to

smoulder, and across the street the wooden overhang of the house opposite came crashing down in flames.

"Help!" they both shouted but there was no one in the street to hear them.

"Get down low. Crawl," said Sam. He remembered his old master, William Kemp, telling him to do this if he were ever caught in a fire.

But it was difficult to crawl with one arm in a sling. And crawl where? The doorway was now ablaze and the upper floor would trap them.

He heard Budge barking from below in the storeroom. The barking went on and on.

Had the dog found something?

"Budge wants us!" he gasped.

He reached out to André, and they stayed close together as they crept back down the stairs to the storeroom.

Budge was still barking. Through the smoke Sam could just see him by the far wall. He crawled towards the dog. Budge caught Sam's sleeve in his teeth and tugged.

"What? What is it?"

And then he saw.

"It's a window! André – it's a window!"

The window had been hidden behind a rough curtain of sacking. Sam wrestled, one-handed, with the catch.

"Let me!" said André. He managed to open the catch, but the wood of the window frame was warped and stuck. He couldn't shift it.

Sam banged it with the heel of his good hand. He couldn't move it either.

Through the small grimy panes of greenish glass they saw a yard with a midden and privy, and thick smoke but no fire.

"Break it!" gasped Sam.

"The panes are too small – we wouldn't get out," said André.

He grabbed a block of wood from the floor and rammed the stiff frame, over and over again.

Budge barked. Flames crackled in the shop above, and smoke rolled down the stairs and engulfed them in choking fumes.

Sam felt dizzy and about to fall when, with one last push from André, the window flew open. Air rushed in, and the storeroom burst into flames behind them.

"Budge – out!"

The dog leapt through the window.

"You next!" said André. He helped Sam to climb up onto the sill.

Sam dropped quickly down on the other side, a fierce pain shooting through his injured arm.

The next minute André landed beside him. "Quick! Let's go!"

They stumbled away from the blazing building.

Budge ran down the length of the yard and turned right along the passage at the end. The boys followed him blindly. Sam had lost all sense of direction.

"Budge will know the way," he said.
"Animals do…"

He broke off in a fit of coughing. It was hard to breathe. He could feel smoke inside his body but could not seem to cough it out.

The dog led them on through alleyways and small streets. Sam knew they were moving gradually uphill, taking mostly lanes that led westward, away from the fire. He put his trust in Budge to get them home.

Budge's lead was trailing. It seemed better to let him run, and to follow him. When they stopped, overcome by fits of coughing, the dog waited for them.

They saw few people on these streets. Most had already escaped, Sam supposed. All around, he heard the hungry voice of the fire and saw flames licking up.

Suddenly the fire seemed to leap. Budge was waiting at the top of an alley when a building nearby exploded in flames. Debris showered down – wood, paper, plaster dust – and smoke rolled between the boys and the dog.

"Quick!" cried Sam.

The two of them ran through the smoke up the alley ahead of them. Budge had been standing, waiting, at the top of it, but he was not there now.

"Budge!" Sam's voice cracked. "Where are you?"

"Budge!" cried André.

The stricken house was blazing, and the flames drove them away, across a road and along another narrow passage. It led uphill – but was that where Budge had gone?

"Budge! Budge!" they called desperately.

Had he been caught in the explosion? They could not stay and search. The fire drove them on, and as they went the smoke thinned and then Sam recognised the Stocks Market, and knew where they were.

"Along here," he croaked. "Poultry, then Cheapside..."

Once again they were among crowds of people and carts. They called for Budge, but he didn't come.

"Perhaps he's gone home," suggested André.

"Yes, of course! That's what he'd do."

They hurried back to Foster Lane.

7

WE MUST GO!

"Where have you been?"

"We've been so worried…"

"Sam! What's happened to your arm?"

Everyone was staring at the boys. Sam
and André stared back. Sam was horrified to
see that Master Giraud had a cut below one
eye and a great bruise on his cheekbone. His
shirt was torn and, around him, the room was
in a mess: a broken window, damage to the
door, smashed plates, hangings pulled down.

Sam and André could only croak and cough in reply to all the questions. Sam's eyes smarted, his face felt sore and his arm hurt. And where was Budge?

André's mother poured weak beer and gave them a cup each. Sam sipped his gratefully. The beer tasted cool and soothed his parched throat.

He whispered, "Is Budge here?" but no one heard him because Mistress Giraud was fussing around André, mourning the state of his new doublet.

"Your good clothes, André! Where have you *been*, the two of you?"

André croaked, "Is Budge here?"

"I don't know!" cried his mother. "I don't care! You stand there in that condition and ask about a dog?"

"We haven't seen him," said Marie.

The two boys looked at each other.

"Lost, then..." said Sam, his chin trembling. André nodded, and his eyes filled with tears.

"Never mind the dog. Where did you *go*?" demanded Paul Giraud angrily. "There is no fire in Lothbury. You went exploring, didn't you? After I told you to come straight home."

They both lowered their eyes and nodded.

"You'll get a beating for this."

"It was my fault," said André. "Not Sam's. He said we shouldn't – " He broke off and began coughing again.

Mistress Giraud intervened. "There is no time for punishment now. We must leave the city. But first I must look at Sam's arm."

Sam flinched as she examined it, but she reassured him. "It's only a fracture. I'll make a splint and bind it, and it will soon heal."

Later, with a new sling and a firm splint on his arm, Sam felt better, and would have enjoyed showing it off and telling the girls about their adventures, if it hadn't been for the loss of Budge.

"Budge saved us," he said. "He found the window."

"And he knew the way home," said André.

"He may still come back," Thérèse said. "He could be frightened and hiding somewhere."

The boys clung to that hope.

But the Girauds were getting ready to leave. Many of the neighbours had already gone, and more were loading up their carts outside. Mistress Giraud had been busy packing belongings while her husband desperately searched Lothbury, Threadneedle Street and Cheapside for the boys.

Thérèse and the little girls told Sam and

André how terrifying it had been when the looters burst into their home.

"They stole gold and silver, and tools, and they attacked Papa and smashed up the workshop," said Thérèse.

"Bijou hissed at the bad men!" said Anne.

"Yes, she did!" exclaimed Marie. "And the neighbours helped us chase them out, and then the soldiers came!"

"Papa hates having to leave," said Thérèse. "He can't believe the fire will come this far. He says the Duke of York and his guards will have things under control soon."

Sam thought of that great relentless beast of a fire, only streets away. But he didn't want to leave either. He wanted to wait for Budge. Supposing Thérèse was right, and his beloved dog was hiding somewhere, frightened to come home?

We can't go without Budge, he thought.

But by late afternoon many of the houses in Foster Lane were already empty, and all the northern gates had long queues of carts and people trailing back.

Sam and André stared out of the landing window.

The city was in flames. Even the clouds were red.

"Budge," whispered Sam, "where are you?"

8

INTO THE FIELDS

It was time to go. Everything that could be carried was packed. Bijou was in a wicker basket, yowling. She would be travelling on one of the two hand-carts that stood outside, already piled high with household goods.

"Please, we *must* look for Budge once more before we go!" begged André.

"Why can't we go and find him?" sobbed Marie.

"There's no time." Their mother was

busy directing Amy and Thérèse, who were carrying a large basket full of linen between them.

Sam could not beg – he was merely a servant – but Paul Giraud knew that of all of them he was the most desperate to find his dog.

"Sam," he said gently, "I think if Budge was alive he would have found his way home by now."

His kind voice made Sam's tears overflow. Sam remembered his last sight of Budge, at the top of that alley, looking back and waiting for them before the smoke engulfed him.

The thought of never seeing him again was unbearable.

"Come." Paul Giraud laid a hand on his shoulder. "We must go now."

Outside, the air was thick with ash. Master and Mistress Giraud took a cart each, Amy lifted a large pack, and everyone else carried what they could, even little Anne.

They had reached Aldersgate when news came that the fire had moved deep into the city.

"The merchants will be fleeing with their gold!" said Master Pryce, their neighbour.

"And we'll lose our homes!" cried Mistress Giraud. "Oh! There's so much we left behind…" She looked sadly at the tottering piles on the carts.

"But we have our lives," said her husband.

They passed through Aldersgate and headed north towards the fields of Islington. People began to flow into every inch of space until the fields were full of carts and makeshift shelters. Some families were simply sitting on the ground surrounded by the few possessions they had been able to carry. There were animals everywhere – chickens in crates, pigs, tethered goats, cows, cats miaowing in baskets and dogs running free.

"But not Budge," murmured Sam.

André shook his head.

"He'll never find us here."

Smoke and ash covered the camp site. Smouldering fragments settled on their hair and clothes and had to be quickly brushed off.

"Will we stay here tonight?" Marie asked.

"We will, my love," said her mother. "Till God puts out the fire, since it seems the people can't."

* * *

In the morning Master and Mistress Giraud improved their makeshift tent while the girls walked to the nearby farm to see if they could buy milk. Sam and André went around the hedgerows collecting blackberries. They worked together, Sam with a bag over his good arm, André doing most of the picking. As they walked back, eating berries, they stopped to stare at the sky above the city walls – one mass of flame from end to end.

"Look at that!"

It was exciting, and when they turned away and saw the fields full of people, and heard the bursts of song and laughter and weeping, Sam knew what an adventure this was and how they'd always remember it, all their lives.

And then he realised something else: that he and André were friends now – or, at least, no longer enemies.

9

OUT OF THE ASHES

All day on Tuesday the people in the fields watched London burn. The sun was blotted out and a constant rain of debris fell on the campsite.

"It feels like the end of the world," said Thérèse.

But when they awoke next morning Master Giraud whispered, "The wind has dropped," and everyone was filled with hope because it was the wind that had been spreading the flames. A dense black cloud of smoke rose high in the air and hung over the city.

"Will we go home now?" asked Anne.

"No, no, *ma petite*! There are still fires to be put out," explained her mother.

They stayed another two nights in the field, but on Friday people began to return to the city, the Girauds among them.

Soon after they passed through Aldersgate, Sam was startled to feel heat coming up through the soles of his shoes.

"My shoes are burning!" he exclaimed.

They came to Goldsmiths' Hall, which was now a burned-out shell, the roof gone, only the walls still standing. And as they walked down Foster Lane, shuffling through hot ash, they saw the ruins of many homes. The street was full of rubble, and smoke was pouring skywards.

"Which house is ours?" cried Mistress Giraud.

It was difficult even to see where Foster Lane ended and Cheapside began, but at last they found the remains of their home and set down their burdens in the ash. Not a scrap of the furniture they had left behind remained whole. Mistress Giraud wept over the loss of almost everything they had owned.

"We will rebuild our home," her husband promised. "Our business, too. And I'll have two young assistants up and coming, I think?" He glanced at Sam and André, who both nodded in agreement.

Master Pryce, who had been gazing at the ashes of his home, next door, said, "We'll work together, the whole street. We'll help each other."

André turned to Sam. "Let's explore!"

"Be careful!" his mother shouted as the boys ran off.

* * *

Cheapside had been burned to the ground.

"Look! You can see the river now!"

London, with its tall buildings and its countless church steeples, was gone. Watling Street, Bow Lane, Friday Street where Sam used to live with Master Kemp – all the way down to the river there was nothing but a smoking wasteland.

"Look at St Paul's!"

The great church was a ruin. Its roof had come crashing down, breaking open the tombs in the crypt, scattering bones and skulls. Stray dogs nosed around them.

Sam hopped about, excited.

"These stones are as hot as an oven!"

They clambered around the ruins until a firefighter chased them away.

Another dog emerged from the crypt as they were leaving. It was lame, with a chewed lead dangling from its collar, and its fur was patchy, singed by fire. *Poor thing*, thought Sam. *It must have been trapped somewhere.*

And then the dog saw him, and with sudden eagerness it hurried towards them. Sam stared.

"It can't be – it *is*! André – it's Budge! It's *Budge*!"

They both dropped to their knees in the ash as the dog reached them. He moved from one to the other of them, panting and licking and making small happy sounds as they stroked and fussed over him.

And his tail kept wagging as if it would never stop.

Plague: A Cross on the Door
Ann Turnbull

In the long, hot summer of 1665, the plague comes to London.
Sam is a servant boy with no family of his own. When his
master dies, Sam is left alone, a prisoner in an empty building
with a cross on the door to mark it as a plague house.

The first of Sam's adventures. Can he escape? And even if he
does, will he be able to survive on London's ravaged streets?

£4.99   ISBN 9781408186879

The Great Fire of London Unclassified: Secrets Revealed!
Nick Hunter

The Great Fire of London Unclassified takes readers
on a journey back in time to uncover the true story
behind London's most destructive fire ever.

From the outbreak of the fire at a bakery on Pudding Lane,
to fire fighting techniques and the meddling Lord Mayor,
readers are taken behind the scenes to see what really happened.
Real-life artefacts and documentation reproduced in full
colour enable readers to build a true and real account
of the Great Fire and how it shaped Britain today.

£10.99   ISBN 9781408193037

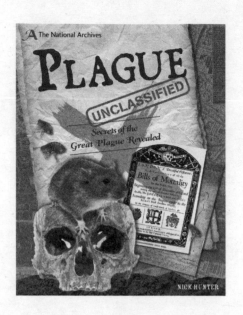

Plague Unclassified: Secrets of the Great Plague Revealed!
Nick Hunter

Focusing on the last British outbreak of plague, the Great Plague of London in 1665, *Plague Unclassified* takes readers on a journey back in time to uncover the story behind the disease.

From what life was like in London during the 1665 outbreak, to where plague came from, how it was spread, and whether it still exists today, real-life artefacts and documentation enable readers to build a true and real account of the bubonic plague and how it shaped Britain today.

£10.99   ISBN 9781408192177